FRIENDS OF ACPL

Y0-EDW-178

For Juanita who lives in Anticoli Corrado

HELEN KAY

A Name for Little-No-Name

**Illustrated by
PETER WARNER**

ABELARD-SCHUMAN
London New York Toronto

© Copyright 1968 by Helen Kay

Library of Congress Catalogue Card Number: 68-13234

Standard Book No: 200.71533.X

Printed in the United States of America

CHAPTER I

CO. SCHOOLS
C702032

Mario had a problem the moment the baby donkey was born.

The mother was called *asina*—just an Italian word for donkey. Like all work donkeys, she followed the farmers to their fields. Every day, except Sunday in the summer, and in the winter when there was school, nine-year-old Mario and his father put their tools into two wooden tubs on each side of *asina's* saddle. Then she led them down the long, winding road to the foot of the mountain where they worked.

At night, Mario, too tired to walk, was carried on her back . . . up . . . up to the top. Sure step followed sure step, all the way home—and at last to bed.

But yesterday and the whole week before the baby was born, Father said, "No one rides *asinà*."

After work, Mario walked. He knew he must because of the baby donkey to be. He blew on his little reed flute. The rhythm moved his tired feet.

Today, in the shed in the animal alley, the new baby lay beside his mother. Mario looked with fresh eyes.

The baby's coat shone with such a warm brown softness, Mario had to reach out and touch. Hands sank into the fluff. It felt so different from *asina*'s scratchy winter coat that needed clipping. Mario was reminded of a downy bird he once had held—all skin and bones and silky feathers.

"I will teach him all the things a good work donkey must know," Mario said.

He would teach him how to walk surefooted down a mountain path, along the very edge of a cliff . . . how to take one small step behind another, how to find a safe spot for a little hoof.

Zig . . . zag . . . to make the trip up the mountain less steep.

Zig . . . zag . . . to make the load easier to carry.

He would teach him how to balance the wooden buckets. Never to budge until they were safe in the saddle. An off-balance load might pull a donkey down the mountainside.

He would teach him how to answer to the prodding stick. Much more—how to answer to the special language that was just for donkeys: "*Arriquaah!*"

That was donkey talk. It meant: "Stop! Go! Come!" depending on the tone of voice. One only used this word with donkeys.

Right now, Mario wanted to speak to the cuddly baby. He wanted to call him by name. But what? "*Asino?*" No, *asina* was for the mother. It would be like saying: "Donkey-donkey, which donkey?"

Both would turn to him with questioning eyes. Mario only wanted the attention of his donkey, the little one. The new one had to have a name of his own. "He needs a name," Mario said.

"A name!" Father cried. "A name for a donkey! No one names a donkey in Anticoli Corrado."

Mario was left to wonder: "Why?"

Father had to go to the fields without his donkey.
Today, he had to carry the tools on his own back.
But first, he pushed a crust of bread into Mario's hand.
"A treat for *asina*," he said.

Since no one gave treats to donkeys, Mario knew
Father was pleased. He was pleased even though the

baby was a colt. In donkeys, females are more important. Not only do they work, but they breed more donkeys.

A white muzzle met Mario's nose. Nose to nose, the fuzz tickled. Mario giggled. The baby rolled over, showing white thighs and a round white belly. But *asina* was nervous. She kicked her heels. Mario leaped aside. He also wanted his donkey to eat and grow.

"I will train him to be a great work donkey," Mario boasted to little brother Carlo who came carrying potato peelings from the kitchen.

"But it takes so long," Carlo said, thinking of the time when he, too, would be old enough to train a donkey.

"Just two years," said Mario. Father had told him long ago. "And I shall name him."

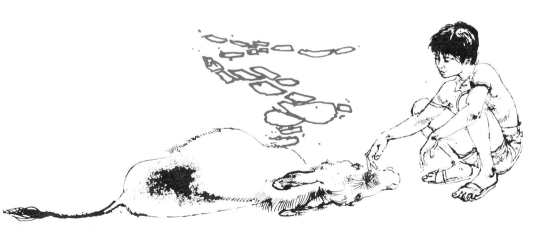

Mother heard him and laughed. "No one names a donkey," she said.

"Why not?" asked Mario.

"Does one name a chicken?" Mother answered with a question.

"But a donkey is not a chicken," Mario said.

"Does one name a pig?" she asked again.

"My donkey is not a pig," Mario said. Why was Mother speaking in riddles?

"We name horses," said Carlo.

Little sister Caterina pulled at Mother's skirts: "Cows, too?" she asked.

"Then call him Little-No-Name," Mother said. "He has a name that is no name."

The newborn colt tried to stand on spindly and unsteady legs. They did not hold, yet. He fell. "See how clever he is," Mario shouted. "He must have a real name."

CHAPTER II

But what kind of name?

On Sunday, the sun shone in the Piazza and everyone knew that Mario had a new donkey. He told them. Besides, he spent the whole morning asking for advice. "What shall I name my donkey?"

"Just call him *Arriquaah*. Come here, move faster," Uncle Filippo answered. "Better still, talk to him with a stick."

Mario did not like the answer. He did not say: "I will not use a stick on my donkey," since that would offend Uncle Filippo, "but. . . ." Uncle Filippo could see that Mario was hurt. He tousled his hair and said, "Nephew, no one names a donkey here. He is too low a character."

"Why not Rosa or Luppeto?" asked Aunt Sophia.

No, Mario shook his head. Rosa and Luppeto were both mules, stubborn and "ignorant." His donkey was a gentle baby.

"Call him *somaro*," suggested the shoemaker.

Even Carlo knew that was just another word for donkey. "*Asina* is a *somara*," he said. "Besides, the new donkey is a baby."

"Then call him *asinello* or *somarello*, little donkey. Boys want to name everything!" The shoemaker was finished with such foolishness.

Mario saw his teacher and rushed to him for help. "Shouldn't everything have a name?" he asked.

"There is a word for everything," the teacher assured him.

"Then why do we not give names to donkeys?" Mario asked.

The teacher looked thoughtfully at Mario. "You have a new donkey?"

"Yes, he was born on Tuesday and he is most beautiful," Mario said, softly.

"Then call him Tuesday, if you wish," the teacher said. "I do not know why we do not name donkeys. Perhaps because donkeys are for drudgery."

Still Mario did not understand.

"Perhaps because life here is so hard for everyone," his teacher said thoughtfully, "we are happy to find something worse off, so we do not name donkeys."

Tuesday! What a name! To Mario, it seemed even the teacher could give no answer.

Mario sang aloud some names he knew: "Midnight, Hector, Rider, Brune, Mora—for Moor." He stopped. They were all horses' names! No, one could not name a donkey for a horse.

Caterina asked: "Why not Violet, Daisy or Mountain Girl?"

Mario snorted: "Names for cows!"

Sadly he left the Piazza. How could *he*, Mario, even think of a name for his donkey, when no one had ever named one before? They would laugh at him. They would say: "Oh, that Mario? He is the boy who names donkeys!"

The baby donkey had long eyelashes and two strong bottom teeth. He was born with them. "He will lose that baby fur and grow as bristly as his mother," Father said as he tied together *asina*'s two front legs. She could hobble, but not wander. The baby was free to roam where he wished, but he would never go far from his mother. He obeyed her every nudge. After he drank her milk, she licked his lips, then she licked his nose, and put her neck on his. So they stood together in a quiet caress.

That is where Serena, the butcher's wife, found them. Even as she came downhill to the animal alley, she was asking, "Is it a male? Will he be for sale when he has more meat on him?"

To Mario, the air seemed suddenly too heavy to breathe. He knew of the trucks that came for the little calves. Now he understood why Mother's answers were like riddles. "Chickens have no names."

Carlo took his hand. He understood, too. "And pigs have no names."

Caterina climbed onto a stump to reach Mario's ear. "Tender little donkeys make *mortadella*—sausage," she said.

Father's answer came loud and clear. "This donkey will be taught by my son to be a work donkey. He is not for sale, *if* . . . they learn to work together."

Mario could breathe again. The air was light again. His donkey was safe! He was too busy counting on his fingers to ask what Father meant when he said: "In a donkey's life there are two great dangers."

Six months? It was April now. In October, he would watch for the truck. He would guard his donkey. Two great dangers? What did Father mean by "*if?*" Of course, they would work together.

CHAPTER III

Summer began when *asina* had her mud-brown coat clipped. She would not need a heavy fur in warm weather. Though she looked strangely nude, her baby was like a woolly lamb.

That first summer, Mario spent all his time with Little-No-Name. He did not wish to miss a single trick. When Mario called, *"Arriquaah!"* gently as one must talk to an infant, Little-No-Name sent one ear in his direction and listened, while he pointed the other . . . where?

Perhaps his mother was calling? Mario wondered: Can he hear differently from each ear? Sometimes the little donkey would flatten both ears. Stretched wide like wings in flight, one on either side of his head, he looked as though his face was all body. He might be a bird about to soar to the sky. But, no, the donkey was grounded on four sturdy legs.

Soon *asina* had to return to work. Father said: "We

will take the baby, too. We will put the *capezza* on
him and he will follow his mother."

Father wound the harness across the baby donkey's
nose and mouth and the back of the head. Another
strap joined the *capezza* to the mother. Now Little-
No-Name followed *asina* wherever she went and
learned to do whatever she did.

Mario looked more closely at those ears! Was one longer than the other? Little-No-Name seemed to hear Mario's voice every time he spoke, but the little donkey did not answer every time.

When Mario came with a treat or just to be near, Little-No-Name heard very well. But if he was to be tied up, one ear stretched farther and farther back. "Learn Little-No-Name, learn to do what I say, when I say it," Mario pleaded. There was always Father's "if". . . .

"One never goes walking with a donkey, without a stick," said Father. "A stick is an accelerator for a donkey."

Mario knew Father's stick was used not to whip *asina*, just to start her off. But who had taught her to go zig . . . zig . . . from side to side, up the mountain

or down? This was the way she wanted to go. For here was a handful of grass, tasty to eat. How could she pass it by? Over there, at the edge of the road, was a handful of poppies, and *asina* liked them, too. Later, when there were berries, she picked them daintily, one at a time with her lips, so slowly. . . . Now her little one followed behind and this was the way he would go. Oh, one cannot hurry a donkey . . . and two donkeys take twice as long.

"Can you whistle, Mario?" Father asked.

Mario pursed his lips. It was different from blowing the flute. He pressed the air between his spaced teeth. A sort of whistle came out. Mario kept trying. He must learn the special sound to use when donkeys drink at the fountain. Mario knew that if he did not whistle, the donkeys would not drink. Father chirped like a bird, a happy bird, that sang and sang and sang. His donkey drank and drank and drank. Mario imitated; Father listened. Mario kept on. It must have been right since *asina* continued to drink. She *shlucked* up the water to his music. When Mario stopped, she stopped, turning to him. . . . She wanted more water. Mario whistled again and she began to drink again. She was a regular reservoir. Twice a day, in the morning when they left through the Piazza and at night when they returned, this was where *asina* drank . . . only here . . . there was no other place.

Mario pushed the baby under the fountain. No, the donkey did not like getting his nose wet. Only the mother drank. Mario ran out of breath. The whistling stopped; the drinking stopped. "Ahhh," Father called as he touched *asina* with his stick. "Ahhh." Then came "*Arriquaah*." The donkey moved.

Mario knew that if *asina* had been a horse, Father would have been more polite. He would have said: "*Passequa*, pass here, if you please." A horse is an animal worthy of respect, but a donkey, a no-name . . . a nothing . . . was just a beast of burden.

Behind Father, with tubs full of tools and vegetables, came *asina* pulling the baby. Then came Mario with a leafy branch—a tickler—to use on the little donkey when he stopped, which was most of the time.

At the animal alley, Father spread hay on the shed floor. "*Stiza*," he said. That meant "stay" to a donkey. Mario murmured softly, "*Stiza*," to his little one.

Mario learned to do all the things Father did. Next summer he would begin to teach his donkey to work. After all, what was a donkey for?

At harvest time, Little-No-Name was six months old and no longer drinking his mother's milk. Now *asina*'s tubs were full of ripe grapes. Mario's mouth watered, but he knew that the little donkey must learn the command: "Don't eat them!" The grapes had to be watched. Both donkeys liked to steal from the tubs. *Asina* knew the silent order of the switch.

Little-No-Name—still "ignorant"—ate everything in sight. He did not care what; flowers, straw, cord, wood, buds, even Mario's own lunch.

Mario thought it was time for the baby to carry something. Oh, nothing heavy. "A heavy load too early will stunt his growth," Father said.

So Mario tied his lunch to the little donkey's rein— a piece of sausage and a crust of bread, wrapped in a red kerchief. As they walked downhill, the little donkey untied a corner and ate the lunch, down to the last crumb. Mario had nothing to eat.

"You are lucky he does not like kerchiefs," Father said, looking at Mario's bright red rag—now empty.

Mario felt very foolish. Little-No-Name blinked black eyes, spread long ears. What could one say to a donkey who loved to tease? "Don't laugh," grumbled Mario, "I'm hungry."

Father took Mario's red rag and spread it on the ground. Everyone put in something from his lunch so that Mario would not go hungry. They also gave him a little pat on the head. After all, they, too, had raised work donkeys. They knew it takes time.

After eating, Mario felt less foolish. He could marvel how neatly the donkey had untied the kerchief. How sly he had been about it all. Soon Mario was tying more bundles to the donkey's back.

"Just a little, just a little, for a little donkey," Father warned.

Even a few blades of grass had to be protected with a swish of the whip. The moment Mario turned his head, the donkey ate all.

The swish in the air became a sting on his hide, when Little-No-Name ate the beans in his mother's buckets. Father was really angry then. "Watch your donkey, Mario," he shouted sternly.

Mario could feel the pain himself, as Little-No-Name leaped, beans spilling from his mouth. Mario took a long silky ear and warned: "You must learn . . . you must learn . . . or you will be sold."

Donkey ears went round and round like the hands of a clock. There was time, Mario hoped. . . .

CHAPTER IV

Early one autumn day as Mario entered the Piazza, he saw the truck.

A little wooden ramp stood in the open door, and Mario knew what was inside without looking.

Mario's lips were dry with fear. He could not whistle. So Father whistled.

While the donkeys drank, Mario felt the driver's eyes on his sturdy little animal. "Hurry! Hurry!" Mario whispered. He knew he must act now to save Little-No-Name.

But it took so long at the fountain. The donkeys drank and drank. Mario tried to hide his little donkey with his own small body, but Little-No-Name was already too big.

It seemed forever before Father moved them along with his swishing stick. They passed the truck. The driver stepped directly into their path. Now Mario could even see inside the truck. Two small donkeys, the same age and size as his own, were tied together.

Mario knew. It was time, now. "*Arriquaah*," he shouted.

Serena, the butcher's wife, was introducing the driver to Father. "This is my brother. He buys donkeys," she said.

Zing . . . Mario's stick was a whip as it went through the air. His donkeys were off. The boy looked back for only a second. He wondered, "What are they saying now?" But it was too late to know. They tore downhill. Mario could neither hear nor see them any longer. Once you start running downhill, everything runs with you. It is hard to stop, even for donkeys surprised by the sudden snap and sting.

To Mario there seemed so little time to save his donkey. He knew that his donkey had given no sign of being good for work. Winter was coming and now they must feed two donkeys instead of one. It would be still another year before Little-No-Name could work—if he could or would learn. Mario was sure, as sure as the hills of Anticoli were high, that Father must sell. His donkey was worthless.

CO. SCHOOLS
C709032

At home, Mario called to Carlo: "Help me . . . the truck for the donkeys. It has come."

Now both boys pulled *asina*. She pulled the little one. They ran to the animal alley. The donkeys had never gone anywhere so fast. The boys pushed the mother into her shed. "*Stiza*," Mario said. "Stay."

He spread straw for her bedding, hay for her supper and slammed the door. He had a plan. "I know a cave, where no one will ever find him." He would save his little donkey. But how can you save a donkey who doesn't want to go?

It was a tug-of-war. They pulled the donkey; the donkey balked. He wanted to stay with his mother. Since a donkey must always look where to place a foot, when he finally began to move, he moved very slowly. As the path became narrower and narrower, he barely moved at all. It seemed to Mario they would never get to the cave.

Under the road, down an embankment, there was no path at all. Here, lay the secret cave. Mario led the way. Now the donkey, sure step following sure step, came behind. Then Carlo, who was no longer even on his feet, came sliding on his seat. At last, they were inside the black hole.

The donkey chewed on dry leaves the boys gathered for his bed and the grass that was his evening meal. By the time Mario and Carlo began to breathe calmly again, Mario's stomach was aching. He was hungry. His belly ached nearly as much as his heart. One was empty—the other, full of fear. Fear for his donkey.

Carlo was only helping his brother, so he could be sensible. He knew that at home, the *palenta* was on the table. He could feel the hot steam of the cornmeal on his face. The taste filled his mouth. His stomach rumbled and grumbled, groaned and moaned. "Let's go home," Carlo begged.

Mario also knew that smell. Suddenly his stomach hurt even more than his heart. It made Mario think, "After all, who would find **the** donkey in the dark in a cave in the middle of the mountain? Surely, Little-No-Name was safe." So the strap which usually held the donkey to his mother was tied around an old vine at the opening. Mario made two double knots. His donkey would stay here, secure, asleep in the belly of the mountain.

Once again the boys passed the Piazza. The truck

was still there. Another little donkey was being led up the plank. The little animal could have been Mario's. It hurt him to watch. He turned and ran home.

Father had finished his evening meal. Two bowls of food were full and waiting. Mario put just one spoonful into his mouth, but he could not swallow. Why was Father so silent? What was he thinking?

Finally Father spoke. "Mario, I was offered 30,000 *lira* for your donkey, today."

Mario's throat was knotted as tightly as he had tied the donkey's rein. So much money for such a little know-nothing.

Father continued, "I told the man, 'My son will be a fine trainer of donkeys. He needs this one to learn how because they are the right age for each other.' "

Mario's head sagged like an emptied balloon. The worry gone, he could no longer hold up his head. He could only think, "The first danger has passed."

But what was that sound? Was that a familiar whinny? Mario ran to open the door.

There stood Little-No-Name—his strap broken and chewed as short as his neck, his ears, held high, listening, listening for Mario's voice.

"Oh," Father laughed. "He did not like the cave."

"How do you know about the cave?" asked Mario.

"I used to hide there, too, when I was a boy," said Father. "It is a good place for boys to hide."

Mario went back to the table. Now he could stuff himself, and satisfy his hunger. Later, the little animal trotted after him to the animal alley. He knew the way back to his mother.

In the Piazza, Mario was relieved to see the truck had gone. He hugged his little donkey. He danced around him. He shouted: "You're safe!"

CHAPTER V

Everyone knows no one can make a donkey work, except his master.

If a donkey is needed to carry hay up the mountain, only his owner can make him haul it. If a donkey is needed to carry a load, only his trainer can lead him. When a donkey is hired, the driver is hired. A donkey is a one-man animal. He will work only for the man who has trained him. And Mario was only a boy.

"Where is Mario?"

With his donkey was the answer. His donkey went wherever Mario went. Little-No-Name followed Mario as though *he* was his mother. Except, of course, to school during the winter and to church on Sunday.

One morning as Mario listened to his teacher he heard, "Mario, we have a guest."

Little-No-Name's head was in the classroom. The rest of him was still outside. He was looking for Mario. The teacher made a joke, "We will now do donkey from a to z—ass to zebra."

Mario did not wait to hear the rest. Head held down with embarrassment, he took his donkey away. How glad he was that Little-No-Name did not wear stripes. Surely he would never hear the end of that. Then both of them would have to run off to the circus.

After church on sunny Sundays, Mario gave the smallest children rides. Caterina first, of course. She was so little. Later Caterina and a friend, one behind the other, rode on the donkey's back. Still later, three small children would ride together. The donkey would trot around the Piazza, gently rocking. When he waited for Mario to change passengers, he sometimes pulled at Caterina's hair ribbon. He loved hair ribbons—just to untie them with his capable lips. It made the children scream with laughter.

When there were no more bows to untie, Little-No-Name would pull Mario's shirt right over his head. Mario could not see. His arms flailed around trying to find the donkey's rein, but the donkey would step out of reach. Then donkey ears went round and round listening to the laughter. He liked its sound.

Serena, the butcher's wife, always watched Mario and his donkey. And she would snort, "Some work donkey."

Mario could hear, but he could not see her. Yet her voice worried him.

The big bow of Serena's Sunday apron teased Little-No-Name. He pulled the strings. The apron fell to the ground. Everyone laughed as she picked it up and retied it. She lost all dignity, and her face grew red with anger.

"That is the strangest little donkey," Uncle Filippo laughed. "More like a clown."

Mario pushed his head out of his shirt. He saw all the laughing faces. He looked lovingly at his donkey. Oh yes, he made life so full of fun.

But Serena scolded, "How can you train a donkey to work when you don't know how?"

Mario did not answer. His heart sank. For this was his fear, too.

By that second harvest Little-No-Name should have known what to eat and what to leave alone; when to stand still and when to go forward or back; what to carry and where to empty a load.

Forty pounds in each tub—that was the load for a work donkey—eighty pounds at a time. It might be dirt for a garden to fill in a rocky ledge, or manure for the grapevines. It could be cement to settle a few stones in a step, or stones to fill a hole in the road. A work donkey must carry the tools to work in the field. He must carry the produce that was ready to bring home, hay and straw, some sacks of grain for the mill, flour for bread, or wood for the fire. Everything that was needed had to be hauled and pulled by the work donkeys.

Little-No-Name knew what to do, but sometimes he dumped the stones down an embankment because red berries at the side of the road asked to be eaten. "*Stiza*," Father shouted while Mario pulled and pleaded.

Sometimes Little-No-Name sat right into a hole he was supposed to fill, because it was cool there. He even ate the hay and slept on the straw he was carrying. How Mario talked and scolded and shouted, and, yes, snapped his whip to keep him working. But when the grapes ripened, then . . . it happened.

Perhaps the donkey had eaten too many grapes on the ground. Perhaps the summer sun had already turned them into wine, and the wine had gone to the donkey's head. Whatever, as Mario walked along, blowing on his flute to keep his own tired legs moving, his donkey simply somersaulted. The fruit spilled into the road, and he calmly ate.

Mario expected to hear Father's warning shout. But Father was already far ahead. He had rounded a bend in the road. He had not seen what happened, yet. The donkey enjoyed himself, while Mario frantically tried to get the fruit back into the tubs. He worked fast, but he could not work faster than the donkey could eat. Nor faster than four donkey hoofs could stamp and trample the beautiful bunches and mash them into pulp.

The sweat and the tears rolled down Mario's face. He knew Father could not forgive this. Little-No-Name was too big now. Mario blamed himself. He should have known. Why hadn't he watched his donkey more carefully? Why had he been so busy with his flute instead of his switch?

Mario did not hear Father come back, but he could feel the cool anger of his long shadow. There was

no shouting, and no spoken warning. The switch stung the donkey's hide. Then Father tied him to his mother as though he were still a baby and "ignorant."

"There is nothing to save," Father said sadly, looking at the grapes in the dusty road. "Someone else will have to teach him, if they can. We will sell him when the truck comes."

What could Mario say? What could he do? Donkey ears were standing straight up! Mario knew in his bones: time had run out.

CHAPTER VI

Two trucks were parked in the Piazza at right angles trailing two large vans, making a corner and a caravan. Mario knew these trucks. He knew the excitement they brought. But he did not care.

The circus had come. Right in the middle of the Piazza, men were putting up a big pole. Soon, the tent, limp as a pile of dirty rags, was spread on the ground. Slowly ropes pulled the tent into position. Mario watched, but he did not feel. "Come on, Mario," Carlo called. He was annoyed with his brother. "The circus is here. There's a show tonight."

But Mario could not join in the fun.

Tomorrow he would have to say "Good-bye" to Little-No-Name.

When the circus family came out of their caravan home and paraded through the street, Mario followed them. But only because this was the way back to the animal alley. He had to get his donkey fed and bedded down. This would be their last evening together.

"Are you going to the circus, Mario?" Serena asked sweetly from her window as Mario passed by.

Her question jolted Mario out of his sadness. Angrily he tugged his donkey out of the circus march and out of her sight. It was all her fault.

MACELLERIA

She would win his donkey. Her brother would come tomorrow and take him away. "How can I save him?" Mario asked Carlo.

"Talk to Father, again," Carlo said, but he was impatient. He wanted to be with the circus. He wanted to watch the clown, the tumblers, the dancing bear, the trained dogs. He wanted to lock up the little donkey for the night and go back to the parade. "We'll think of something later," he promised.

Mario gave his donkey a bigger pile of straw to sleep on. He gave him extra supper. The donkey settled himself and blinked black eyes at his master.

Carlo took Mario's hand and pulled him back to the Piazza to the circus tent, to a seat on a hard bench. Everybody was already there. They were seated behind Mario: Father and Mother, Caterina and Uncle Filippo. Aunt Sophia, the shoemaker, even Serena. But Mario did not see them.

When two trained dogs came out and somersaulted one over the other, then the other over him, Mario only thought of his unruly little donkey and his long lashes. When the dancing bear waltzed with his trainer, Mario remembered how on sunny Sundays he led his little donkey around the Piazza giving the children rides. For one moment only, Mario forgot that donkey.

The trapeze artist twisted and turned and leaped through the air into the arms of another acrobat. Mario jumped out of his seat with excitement. His hands clapped as the whole circus family climbed one on top of the other into a giant pyramid. Mario was captured by the excitement. He forgot Little-No-Name.

Just then . . . a little donkey entered the ring. He ran round and round the arena, looking, looking. The audience laughed and called: "A trained donkey!"

Mario could not believe what he saw. "Carlo," he asked, "is it?"

Carlo asked Caterina, "Is it?" Caterina was too busy watching, to say.

The clown was as surprised as Mario. Donkey ears were turning, turning like antennae. One ear was listening for his master's voice. The other was listening to what the old clown was shouting. Alas, he did not speak donkey talk. But Mario did. He was on his feet, calling, "*Arriquaah!*"

Little-No-Name heard. He came running. Now Mario's face was as red as the clown's—from embarrassment. He was ashamed of his troublesome donkey. He could see—he could feel—Little-No-Name was heading for even more trouble.

"*Arriquaah!*" Mario called again.

Little-No-Name ran in front of the dancing bear and tripped him. He sped past the acrobatic dogs and they tumbled to the floor. At last, Little-No-Name was beside him. Mario grabbed his rein and held. Why was everybody laughing? Little-No-Name nuzzled. Now that Mario's shirt was right in front of the donkey's two big bottom teeth, he grabbed and lifted it over Mario's head. Mario stood there

with hands in air, holding tight to the rein. The donkey brayed, and spread his ears.

Why weren't they scolding his donkey? Why was the audience applauding? Such a noise they made. They were calling: "Buffo! Buffo!"

Mario could not see, but he could hear. "He is a regular buffoon. He is a clown of a donkey."

Mario was not embarrassed anymore. He understood. They were laughing at his donkey. He pulled his shirt down. Now he could see, too. The clown was bowing. The show was over. His donkey was the star. Afterward, everyone came to praise him.

"Buffo," said the shoemaker. "You are a clown."

"Buffo," said Uncle Filippo, "you are for laughter."

Father was standing there, smiling. He said: "I guess we cannot sell such a popular fellow. He came straight to you, just as you ordered."

Mario put his face right into the donkey's coat, rough and bristly now. He did not want Father to see his tears. They had another chance—he and his donkey—together.

Father said very gently: "I think, Mario, the village has named your donkey."

"Buffo," Mario said softly, into trembling donkey ears. Mario liked the name. It made him smile. It fitted his donkey.

And that is how a donkey first earned a name in Anticoli Corrado. No one had ever thought of it before.